Karen, Hannie, and Nancy:
The Three Musketeers

**Look for these
and other books about Karen
in the
Baby-sitters Little Sister series:**

Little Sister

Karen, Hannie, and Nancy:
The Three Musketeers

Ann M. Martin

Illustrations by Susan Tang

A
LITTLE APPLE
PAPERBACK

SCHOLASTIC INC.
New York Toronto London Auckland Sydney

For Dick Krinsley

Activities by Nancy E. Krulik
Activity illustrations by Heather Saunders

ISBN 0-590-45644-X

Copyright © 1992 by Ann M. Martin. All rights reserved. Published by Scholastic Inc. APPLE PAPERBACKS is a registered trademark of Scholastic Inc. BABY-SITTERS LITTLE SISTER is a trademark of Scholastic Inc.

12 11 10 9 8 7 6 5 4 3 2 1   2 3 4 5 6 7/9

Printed in the U.S.A.   40

First Scholastic printing, August 1992

KAREN

Summer Vacation

I banged through the front door of Mommy's house. I banged into the kitchen. I dropped my things all over the floor — pencils, papers, an old workbook, three flower erasers, two sticks of gum, a papier-mâché rabbit, and a folder full of paintings.

It was the last day of school.

I had cleaned out my desk.

"Goodness, Karen," said Mommy. She and Andrew were in the kitchen. They had been shelling peas. Now they were looking at my mess. (Andrew is my little brother.

1

He is only four-going-on-five. I am seven. I am his big sister.)

"I will clean it up. Don't worry," I told Mommy. Then I stood on a chair. I sang, "School's out! School's out! Teacher wore her bloomers out!" I smiled at Andrew.

But he frowned. "What does that mean?" he asked. "What are bloomers?" He opened a pea pod and popped out the peas.

"You know, I do not have any idea," I said. "I just heard some big kids singing that today. I heard them sing something else, too. They sang, 'No more pencils, no more books! No more teachers' dirty looks!' I do not like that song, though. Ms. Colman never, ever gave me a dirty look. She is much too nice."

I hopped off the chair. I began to scoop up my mess.

I am Karen Brewer. I have blonde hair and some freckles. I have glasses. Two pairs. I wear my blue glasses when I read, and my pink glasses when I do other things.

I have two best friends. Their names are Nancy Dawes and Hannie Papadakis. They are a *little* older than I am. They are almost eight. Nancy lives next door to Mommy. Hannie lives across the street from Daddy and one house down. (My parents are divorced. They do not live in the same house anymore. But they live in the same town. Stoneybrook, Connecticut. I was born here.)

Hannie and Nancy and I call ourselves the Three Musketeers. We are going to be best friends forever and for always. I had big summer plans for my friends and me. We were going to stay together as much as possible. We were going to spend every day together. (We are such good friends that we have matching friendship bracelets. I made Nancy's, Nancy made Hannie's, and Hannie made mine. They are gigundoly beautiful.)

These are some of the things the Three Musketeers wanted to do over summer vacation: ride our bikes, roller skate, go to the playground, swim, do arts and crafts, and read, *read*, READ!

We have ninety-one days of summer vacation.

Hannie and Nancy and I were going to do something else together. Something exciting and extra-fun.

We were going to take a trip.

Not by ourselves, of course. Daddy and his family were going to spend two weeks at a lake. Daddy said I could invite friends along. So Hannie and Nancy were coming to the lake with me.

Andrew was not bringing friends, though. That is because he is *so* young. He cannot even read yet. But he wants to learn. He is always saying, "Teach me! Teach me!"

I am glad I can read. I am glad the Three Musketeers can read together sometimes. And I am especially glad to be one of the Three Musketeers.

KAREN

Karen Brewer

My parents were not always divorced. They were married for awhile. They were married long enough to have Andrew and me. But after a few years, they decided they did not love each other enough to stay married. That was when they decided to get divorced. (Of course, they still loved Andrew and me.)

Mommy and Daddy and Andrew and I had been living in a gigundo house. It was Daddy's big house. He had grown up in it.

When the divorce happened, Mommy moved out. She took Andrew and me with her. We moved into a much smaller house.

Do you want to know something interesting? Mommy and Daddy got married again — but not to each other. Mommy married Seth Engle. He is my stepfather now. Daddy married Elizabeth Thomas. She is my stepmother now. I have two families.

These are the people in the little-house family: Mommy, Seth, Andrew, and me. The pets are Rocky and Midgie, Seth's cat and dog, and Emily Junior. She's my rat. I live at the little house most of the time. I like my little-house family.

The rest of the time I live at Daddy's with my big-house family. Andrew and I live there every other weekend, on some holidays and vacations, and for two weeks during the summer. These are the people in my big-house family: Daddy, Elizabeth,

Elizabeth's kids, Nannie, Emily Michelle, Andrew, and me. Elizabeth's kids are Sam, Charlie, David Michael, and Kristy. They are my stepbrothers and stepsister. Sam and Charlie are in high school. David Michael is seven like me. And Kristy is thirteen. She is a very good baby-sitter. I just love Kristy. Nannie is Elizabeth's mother, so she is my stepgrandmother. And Emily Michelle is my adopted sister. Daddy and Elizabeth adopted her from a country called Vietnam. Emily is two and a half. She does not say much yet, but she is learning to talk. (I named my rat after her.)

Also at the big house are some pets. Boo-Boo is Daddy's mean, old cat. You have to be careful with him. He scratches. Shannon is David Michael's puppy, and he is very sweet. He licks me with his tongue. I call that puppy-kissing. Crystal Light the Second and Goldfishie are two goldfish. They belong to Andrew and me. They do not do much. Mostly, they swim and eat and garble their mouths around.

I have special names for my brother and me. I call us Andrew Two-Two and Karen Two-Two. (Once, my teacher read a book to our class. It was called *Jacob Two-Two Meets the Hooded Fang.* That's where I got the idea for our names.) Andrew and I are two-twos because we have two of so many things. Two houses, two families, two mommies, two daddies, two cats, and two dogs. Plus, I have two best friends. And I have two bicycles, one at each house. (Andrew has a tricycle at each house.) I have clothes and books and toys and games at each house. I even have two stuffed cats. They look just the same. Moosie stays at the big house, Goosie stays at the little house. This is nice because Andrew and I do not have to pack much when we go from one house to the other.

Of course, I do not have two of *every*-thing. I do not have two rats, so I miss Emily Junior when I am at Daddy's. Also,

I miss my little-house family. But then when I am at the little house, I miss my big-house family.

I hardly ever miss my best friends, though. The Three Musketeers are together forever. All for one and one for all!

Nancy Dawes

Hello, my name is Nancy Dawes. Really, it is Nancy Jane Dawes, but no one ever calls me Nancy Jane. Not even my parents. (I am not sure why they bothered with that extra name.)

I am seven and three quarters years old.

I live with my mother and father here in Stoneybrook, Connecticut. There are no other people in my family. I mean, no other people who live in our house. I do not have even one brother or sister, which is a shame.

I do have two best friends, though. They are Karen Brewer and Hannie Papadakis. Hannie is seven and three quarters years old, like me. Karen is younger. She just turned seven. Hannie and Karen and I are the Three Musketeers. We go to school together. We go to Stoneybrook Academy.

Hannie and Karen are lucky. They have brothers and sisters. Hannie has one of each. Karen has *two* sisters and *four* brothers. She does not get to live with all of them all the time, though. That is because she's a two-two.

This is what I look like: light brown hair, blue eyes, and freckles. If I had a sister, I wonder if she would look like me. Would a brother look like me? Karen and her brother Andrew look very much alike. But Hannie does not look like either her sister or her brother. She looks a little like her father, though.

The second floor of my house is the bedroom floor. We have three bedrooms.

The big one is for Mommy and Daddy. The middle-sized one is mine. The small one does not belong to anybody. Sometimes guests sleep in it. Sometimes Mommy sews in it. Sometimes Daddy writes letters in it. But a bedroom should belong to someone. Like a baby. Like my baby brother or sister. Then I would not have to be an only child.

Do you know what? I do not have any grandmas or grandpas, either. (My family is kind of small.) But I do have a friend I call Grandma B. Grandma B is *really* old. She lives in Stoneybrook Manor where a lot of other old people live. She is a very good friend of my family's. Grandma B even spends holidays with us, like Rosh Hashanah and Yom Kippur and Passover. She does not seem like most old people to me. She likes to listen to music and dance. Sometimes she sings.

I like to do those things, too. I plan to be an actress one day. I think Karen and I

12

might star in something together. Like maybe *The Nancy Dawes Show*. Hannie could be in it, too, if she wanted.

My house is an extra-quiet place. No brothers or sisters or grandparents. And for a long time: no pets. We did not even have a fish. Once, a moth flew into my bedroom. I named him Bob, but he did not stay. But now I have my first pet. He is a kitten named Pokey! Hannie and Karen each have several pets. Karen has a rat of her very own. At her father's house, she has a goldfish, too. Plus, a dog and a cat live at her mother's house, and another dog and cat live at her father's. Hannie and her brother and sister have three pets.

My house is the quietest one I know. But a baby would take care of that. And *I* could take care of a baby. I am sure I could learn how to change diapers and stuff. A nice name for a little boy would be Biff Bartholomew. A nice name for a little girl would be April May.

Did I say that I love my parents very, very much? Well, I do. I do not even care that they are quiet people who like a quiet house. They are the best, best mommy and daddy, and I am glad they are mine. I wonder if they would let me change my name to Rodelia, for when I am an actress.

4

Hannie

Hannie Papadakis

Hey, it's me, Hannie Papadakis! Do you know what kind of name Papadakis is? It's Greek. So I am Greek. But I was born here in Stoneybrook, Connecticut. And my parents were born in the United States. But my *grand*parents, all four of them, were born in Greece. I have never been to Greece, but maybe someday I will go there. Someday when I am a world traveler and I am on my way to Italy and China.

Hannie is not my real name. My real name is Hannah. I like Hannie better —

15

even though Hannah is spelled the same whether you start at the beginning or the end, whether you spell it forward or backward. Always the same. H-A-N-N-A-H. My mother says not many names are like that. I can only think of three others. Eve, Ava, and Otto. (There must be more.)

I have an older brother and a younger sister. My brother is Linny. He is nine-going-on-ten. (Oh, by the way, I am seven-going-on-eight.) Linny is *usually* a nice brother, except that sometimes he teases. My sister is Sari. She is two-going-on-three. She used to be a sweet little baby. Now she is a PAIN IN THE NECK. She is always coming into my room and messing up my stuff. I yell at her, but then she comes back and does it again.

Our family has three pets. They are a dog, a kitten, and a box turtle. Their names are Noodle the Poodle, Pat the Cat, and Myrtle the Turtle. Myrtle was our first pet ever. (She *might* be a boy, but we are not sure.) Then we got Noodle. And then we got Pat.

Guess what. I am a Musketeer. I have two best friends, and we try to stick together, so we call ourselves the Three Musketeers. My friends are Karen Brewer and Nancy Dawes. When Karen stays at her father's house, she lives across the street from me. Mostly she is at her mother's house, though. And her mother's house is right next door to Nancy's. Karen and Nancy are lucky. I wish I lived nearer to them.

I am glad summer vacation is here. I do not like school too much. I would rather be with my friends and play outdoors. Nancy likes school, and Karen loves school, but not me. Here are the things I like to do: play tag, swim, ride my bike, run races, read. Karen and Nancy and I all like to read.

A few days ago, Mommy took Linny and Sari and me to the library. I sat on the floor

in the children's room. I looked and looked and looked. After a long time, I chose ten books. That is the most you can check out at one time. This summer I am going to try reading the books by an author named Carol Ryrie Brink. I found two of her books. They are *Baby Island* and *Caddie Woodlawn*. I am going to read another book called *Sarah, Plain and Tall*. (It is by someone named Patricia MacLachlan.) And I am going to read some of the stories about Paddington Bear. Karen likes those books. They are by a man named Michael Bond.

Since I like to read, maybe I will be a writer when I grow up. (It is too bad I cannot be a reader. I do not think you can earn money just by reading.) I think I will be a writer who travels around the world. When I get tired of that, I will swim in the Olympics. I will win gold medals. Then I will stop to write a book about being an Olympic swimmer. After I finish the book, I will be a gardener for awhile and then a painter. Then I will build two houses. One for me, and one for someone else. (I do not know who.) Then maybe I will write another book or two.

Daddy says I need to concentrate. Mommy says my mind flits around like a butterfly. It never thinks the same thought for very long. I cannot help that. Anyway, I am glad my mind flits. If it did not, I might get bored. Karen's mind flits around sometimes, too. So does Nancy's. Maybe that is one reason we are the Three Musketeers.

Do you know what? I really wish my family had an ice-cream maker.

KAREN

The Three Musketeers

Here is a good thing about summer: You do not have to wear too many clothes. In the summer I can get dressed in a flash. Underwear, shorts, shirt. If I am not going to leave my yard, those are the only clothes I have to put on. (If I am going to leave the yard, then I have to put on sandals, or maybe socks and sneakers.)

I can get dressed in about ten seconds.

On the first whole day of summer vacation, I wore a pair of red shorts and my new blue T-shirt with the tropical fish on the front. I asked Mommy to time me while I got dressed.

"Okay!" I called to her when my clothes were laid out.

"Go!" said Mommy.

"Stop!" I called when I finished dressing.

"Eight seconds!" said Mommy.

"Yes! A new record! This summer I am going to see if I can beat that record. I will try to dress in *seven* seconds."

"Karen?" said Andrew. He poked his head in my room. "What are you going to do today?" He was still in his pajamas. He has not set a dressing record that I know of.

"Play with my friends," I said.

"Play what?"

Hmm. Good question. We could do so *many* things. We could play tag and statues. We could sit in the yard and wait for the mail truck and the ice-cream truck. We could go to Melody Korman's house. (Melody has a swimming pool.) We could ride our bikes. We could go to the playground. We could paint pictures.

"Huh, Karen?" said Andrew.

"I am not sure yet," I told him. "I better call Nancy and Hannie. Then I will decide."

I stood in the kitchen and dialed Hannie's number. I watched an ant crawl across the floor. It crawled over my foot. I could hardly feel it. "Hannie?" I said when she picked up the phone. "Are you ready?"

"Ready for what?"

"Our first summer day together. The Three Musketeers."

"Oh, yeah."

"Can you come over right away?"

"I think so." (Hannie has to ask someone to drive her to my little house. Nancy can walk, since she lives just next door.)

"Great. I'll see you soon," I said. "And bring your doll." Then I telephoned Nancy.

"It's me! Can you come right over? Hannie is on her way."

"Yup," answered Nancy. "What are we going to do today?"

"I am still deciding. Maybe you better ride your bike over, just in case. And bring your doll."

I hung up the phone. I looked around for the ant, but it was gone.

I sat on our front steps with my doll. I watched Nancy ride her bike out of her garage next door. I watched her ride it down her driveway, along the sidewalk, and up our driveway. She parked her bike by the fence.

"Hi, Musketeer!" she called. She took her doll out of her bike basket.

"Hi, Musketeer!"

Nancy sat next to me on the steps. We waited for Hannie.

"I broke my dressing record today," I said. "Eight seconds."

"Cool."

Soon Hannie arrived. Her mother dropped her off.

"Yea! The third Musketeer is here!" I said. "Okay, you guys. Get ready for today. We are going to be very busy. We have a lot to do."

"Karen, it is vacation," Hannie reminded me.

"I know. Now pay attention, Muske-teers."

Nancy

The Doll Sisters

My alarm clock looks like a cat. It makes three different sounds: purr, growl, meow. You can set it to the sound you want. Usually, I set it to *meow*. Then the clock wakes me up by saying, "Meow, meow, meow!"

On the first day of summer vacation I did not need my meow-clock. I did not need Mommy to rap on my door and say, "Nancy! Time to get up!" All I needed was the sunlight. When it shone through my window, it woke me up gently. I lay in my bed and thought about the Three Musketeers. I wondered what Karen would plan for us to do.

Karen just loves to make plans.

I yawned. I stretched. I slid out of bed. I put on my new sundress.

Then I stepped into the hallway. I peeped in Mommy and Daddy's room. It was empty. The bed was made. I looked at my watch. Almost eight-thirty. Yipes! Daddy had probably already left for work.

I ran downstairs. Before I reached the steps I passed Mr. Nobody's room, the room that should belong to a baby brother or sister. We could put a crib in the corner by the window. We could get a chest and fill it with toys. Or I could give the baby my own toy chest, the one Daddy painted with pictures of Paddington Bear and Madeline.

I sighed.

We did not have a baby, so I should stop thinking about cribs and toy chests.

"Happy first day of summer!" said Mommy when I walked into the kitchen.

28

She fixed cantaloupe and strawberries for a special treat.

"Mommy?" I began. I was going to tell her how much I wanted a brother or sister. But I decided not to. "Nothing," I said. "Thank you for the strawberries."

Brrrring! rang the phone.

"I'll get it!" I leaped out of my chair. I grabbed the phone. Karen was calling. And she told me to bring my doll to her house.

I knew which doll she meant. Not just any doll. *The* doll. Merry. Hannie and Karen and I have triplet dolls. They look just the same. We bought them at a toy store. I named mine Merry, Karen named hers Terry, and Hannie named hers Kerry.

Together they are the Doll Sisters.

We decided that the Three Musketeers *needed* the Doll Sisters. We could play with them a lot. We could make sister outfits and sister jewelry for them. There is just one problem with the Doll Sisters. Really, the problem is with Terry. Karen has only one sister doll. Not two. Terry is not a two-two.

And sometimes Karen forgets to bring Terry from the big house to the little house, or from the little house to the big house. Then she cannot play with her for awhile. Oh, well.

Karen said to ride my bike over to her house, so I did. I put Merry in the basket. She likes bike-riding.

Soon the Musketeers were together and so were the Doll Sisters.

"First," said Karen, "we are going to build a house for the Doll Sisters."

"Cool!" I said.

"Yeah, cool," agreed Hannie.

We found a whole pile of big cardboard boxes in Karen's garage. I pulled out the largest one. "The Doll Sisters share a bedroom," I said. "This big box should be the bedroom."

"We will paint it pink," said Karen.

"This little box can be the bathroom," announced Hannie.

"We will paint it yellow," said Karen.

We dragged the boxes into the backyard.

We stuck them together with masking tape. Then we cut out windows. Then we cut out doors.

Then we got bored.

And hungry.

"Time for lunch," said Karen.

Hannie

Stoneybrook Playground

Karen's mother let us eat lunch at the picnic table in the backyard. That was terrific. The not-so-terrific part was that Andrew wanted to eat with us. And Mrs. Engle said he could. (Mrs. Engle is Karen's mother.)

Karen and Andrew sat on one side of the table. Nancy and I sat on the other. The benches are tippy. If anybody has to stand up, he is supposed to warn the person he's sitting next to, so the bench will not flip over. If you sit on one of those benches alone, you better sit in the middle.

For lunch we ate sandwiches and Pop-sicles. My Popsicle was lime. It turned my tongue green. I stuck my tongue out at An-drew. "Look! I am an alien!" I cried. "I am from Mars."

Andrew looked as if he might either laugh or cry. But instead he just said, "No, you aren't." He is no fun.

He is better than Sari, though.

When we had licked our Popsicle sticks clean, I leaped to my feet.

"Hey!" cried Nancy as she slid to the ground. "Hannie!"

"Sorry," I said. "I forgot to warn you. But I have an idea. Listen."

"No, *I* have an idea," Karen answered. "It is now time for the Three Musketeers to go to the playground."

Well, that was not what I was going to suggest. But it was a good idea.

"Can I come, too?" asked Andrew.

"Nope. Just the Three Musketeers," Karen answered.

We told Mrs. Engle where we were going. Then we hopped on our bikes. (I borrowed one from David Michael.) We are allowed to ride to the playground all by ourselves. It is called the Stoneybrook Playground, and it is not too far away. Get this. Nancy and Karen and I helped build the playground. We really did. Everyone in town helped. Now we have a wonderful place to play.

A lot was going on at the playground. There was a special summer program. A counselor was teaching a group of kids how to play soccer. Another counselor was reading to some kids. And another counselor was teaching arts and crafts.

"Cool!" I cried. "Let's try everything." So we did.

We played soccer for awhile. Then we listened to a funny story called *Pop Corn and Ma Goodness*. Then we made boxes out of Popsicle sticks. Also, we tried to make lanyards, but that was hard. None of us could

figure out what to do with a finished lanyard anyway.

"Use it as a keychain," suggested the counselor.

"I do not have any keys," I replied.

So I made another box from Popsicle sticks. "You know what?" I said to Nancy and Karen. "I will paint my boxes. I will put glitter on them. They will be jewelry boxes. They will make good presents. I think I will give one to my aunt. And I will make some jewelry to go in it. Did I tell you that my aunt is getting married? Well, she is. In Greece. Someday I am going to visit Gr — "

Karen interrupted me. "Hey, in three weeks we leave for the lake."

"Yes!" I cried. Karen's daddy was taking a bunch of people on a trip. We were going to stay in a cabin on a lake. The lake is named Shadow Lake. (I do not know why.) I had not been to Shadow Lake before. But I was glad I was going. Two weeks with no Sari.

"At the lake," said Karen, "we can go swimming."

"Maybe we can ride in a boat," I added.

I looked at Nancy. I waited for her to say something. But she was busy with a pink-and-orange lanyard. Maybe she had not heard me.

When Nancy finished her lanyard, we went home. The Three Musketeers had to split up for dinner. That was okay. We would see each other bright and early the next morning.

KAREN

Hop on Pop

"Yea! Hurray! It is time to take," I sang, "all of my things to Shadow Lake!"

I was so happy. Our trip would begin the next day. I was in my room at the little house. I was packing my suitcase for the trip.

The next morning, Mommy would drive Andrew and Nancy and me to the big house. Then we would leave on our adventure.

"Let me see," I said. I counted shirts into a pile on the bed. "One, two, three, four, five —"

38

"Karen?" said Andrew.

"Wait. I am counting. One, two, three, four, five — "

"Karen?"

"Just a minute! One, two, three, four, five — "

"Karen?"

"WHAT?"

"Will you teach me how to read?"

"Not now."

"Please?"

"I said not now."

"Pretty please?"

"Andrew! I will teach you to read over the summer. How is that?"

"Do you promise?"

"Yes. I promise. I promise that by the end of the summer you will be able to read *Hop on Pop* all by yourself. But only if you will leave me alone right now. I am trying to pack."

"Okay," agreed Andrew. He ran downstairs.

Good. Now I could concentrate. I sat on

the bed. I counted the shirts again. Then I counted pairs of socks. When my clothes were packed, I remembered that I would need to bring toys and books to the lake.

I looked at the stuffed animals and dolls on my bed. "I will bring you, Goosie," I said. "And of course you, Terry." The Three Musketeers were bringing the Doll Sisters. We could not just go off and leave them.

But I did have to leave Emily Junior behind.

"Why?" I had asked Daddy. "You get to bring Boo-Boo and Shannon."

"That is different," said Daddy. "They would have no one to take care of them. But Mommy and Seth can take care of Emily Junior for you. Besides, you know how Nannie feels about rats."

I knew. "Sorry, Emily," I said to her. "No vacation for you." But I was still excited about our trip.

9

Nancy

Homesick

M*eow-meow-meow-meow-meow*. My alarm clock was going off. At first, I could not figure out why. I thought, It is still summer vacation. This is not the first day of school.

"Nancy!" Mommy called. "Time to get up. Today is the day."

Then I remembered Shadow Lake. Soon I would be going away with Karen's family. For two weeks.

I did not want to go.

My suitcase was packed. Merry was ready for the trip. Karen had said we could swim and fish and bike and ride in boats.

But I did not want to go.

At breakfast that morning I said to Mommy and Daddy, "I do not feel very well. I think maybe I better not go to the lake."

"You are homesick," said Daddy.

"How can I be? I am still at home."

"You know what I mean."

I nodded. "Can't I stay here? Please?"

"Is that what you really want to do?" asked Mommy.

"Yes," I said. Then I thought of Hannie and Karen swimming and having fun together at the lake — while I stayed in Stoneybrook. They would be the Two Musketeers, and I would be the One Lonely Musketeer. "No," I said to Mommy. "Oh, I don't know."

"Why don't you try it?" asked Daddy. "We can always drive to the lake and get you if you *really* want to come home."

"Okay," I said in a tiny voice.

Before I knew it, Karen rang our doorbell.

I burst into tears.

Mommy and Daddy gave me hugs.

"What's wrong?" asked Karen when I answered the door.

"I am going to be homesick," I wailed.

"At the lake?" said Karen. "No, you will not. You will be with Hannie and me. The Three Musketeers will be together. That is all that matters."

"But I will not be at home!"

"Even the Doll Sisters will be at Shadow Lake," said Karen.

"That is another thing. I do not like the name of the lake. It sounds scary. I bet the lake is haunted. We will probably run into ghosts."

"Why don't you stay at home then?" said Mommy.

"No. I want to be with my friends."

"Then get in the car," said Karen.

"No. I want to stay at home."

Karen smiled. Then she laughed. So did Mommy and Daddy. So did I. I knew I was being silly. It was time to leave.

43

But first I would have to say good-bye.

I put my arms around Mommy's waist. "I love you," I said. "I will see you in fourteen days. Remember to return my library books."

"Okay, sweetie."

I put my arms around Daddy's waist. "Good-bye. I love you. The next time you see me I will be two weeks older."

"I probably will not even recognize you."

"Oh, Daddy," I said.

Daddy helped me carry Merry and my suitcase to Karen's car. I climbed into the backseat next to Karen. Daddy talked to Mrs. Engle for a few minutes. Then we drove away. Soon I could see Karen's big house. Across the street was Hannie. She was saying good-bye to *her* family.

Hannie

B-I-N-G-O

"Here they come!" I called, "I see the car!"

I was in my front yard with Mommy and Daddy and Linny and Sari. Karen's car was driving down the street.

"It is time to leave for Shadow Lake," I added.

"Yes!" cried Linny. "All *right!*" Linny was going to Shadow Lake, too. He is a friend of Karen's brother David Michael. David Michael had invited two friends to go on the trip, just like Karen had. I sort of wanted to be grown-up and go away from my *whole* family, but now I could not. Oh, well. At least I would leave Sari the pest behind. I knew I would not miss her at all. I was going on a vacation from Sari. A Sari vacation.

"Well, 'bye!" said Linny to Mommy and Daddy.

"Hey, don't I get a kiss?" asked Mommy.

"Not out here in public," hissed Linny. "Everyone will see."

"I will kiss you," I said grandly. I stood on tiptoe. I leaned up and kissed Mommy. Then I leaned up and kissed Daddy. Daddy was holding Sari in his arms. I did not kiss Sari. I said to her. "Do not go in my room while I am away. And do not touch my stuff!"

"Hannie," warned Daddy.

I sighed. "Sorry, Sari," I said. Then I added, "Good-bye."

Linny and I started to run across the yard.

I heard a voice behind me. It was Sari. "Hannie! Hannie!" she called.

I turned around. Sari was reaching her arms toward me. She was almost falling. Daddy had to hold onto her tightly.

I ran back to Sari and gave her a kiss. Then Linny and I carried our suitcases and stuff across the street.

Everybody was in Karen's driveway. Karen and her daddy and her two mommies and all her brothers and sisters and their friends and Nannie and Nancy.

"Hello!" I called.

The Brewers' van was broken, so we had to take *three* cars to the lake. That just shows how many people were going on the trip. Karen's daddy was driving the car I rode in. I rode with him and Karen and Nancy and two of Kristy's friends who are very excellent baby-sitters. Their names are Dawn and Stacey. The Three Musketeers rode together in the backseat. Dawn and Stacey and Mr. Brewer sat in the front seat.

As soon as Mr. Brewer pulled out of the

driveway, Karen said, "Daddy? How many minutes until we get there? Is this going to be a long trip?"

"A few hours," he said.

"I like long car rides," said Nancy. "Let's play games."

"Like what?" I asked.

"Like Riddle Me Ree. Listen to this. Riddle me, riddle me, riddle me ree. I see something you don't see, and the color of it is . . . yellow. What is it?"

"I hope it is in the car," I said. "If it is outside, we have probably already passed it. We will never see it."

"Of course it is in the car," said Nancy. "Look for it."

Karen and I looked. We guessed and guessed. The answer was my barrette!

"How about singing songs?" said Stacey from the front seat. " 'Bingo' is a good one. Let's sing 'Bingo.' "

So we sang, "There was a farmer had a dog, and Bingo was his name-o. B-I-N-G-O, B-I-N-G-O, B-I-N-G-O, and Bingo was

his name-o. There was a farmer had a dog and Bingo was his name-o." On that second verse, we clapped instead of singing the letter B. After that, we clapped for B and I. By the last verse we were clapping like this: clap, clap, clap-clap, clap.

As soon as we finished the song, Karen said, "Daddy, are we almost there yet?"

"No."

So Stacey taught us some new songs.

Finally Karen said, "Daddy, are we almost there yet?"

And he said . . . "Yes!"

KAREN

The Secret Garden

Yesterday morning I woke up in Stoneybrook, in my bed in the little house. This morning I woke up in a bunk in a cabin at Shadow Lake.

Daddy's cabin is very wonderful. It is not really a cabin. It is a house. And it is pretty big. (Andrew was not happy when he first saw it. He thought we were going to stay in an old-fashioned log cabin. He cried a little bit.)

In the cabin are four bedrooms. Two are tiny and two are huge. The kids are sleeping in the huge bedrooms, girls in one, boys in the other. *Six* bunk beds are in each room. The girls fill up eleven of the beds: Hannie, Nancy, me, Emily Michelle, Kristy, and Kristy's six friends, the Baby-sitters. (There are only six boys in the other room. Each of them gets a whole *bunk* to himself. The boys are gigundoly lucky.)

Here is what is in back of our cabin: woods. Here is what is in front: Shadow Lake. We have our very own dock. We can jump off the dock and go swimming.

Kristy and her friends are baby-sitting all us younger kids. That first day Mary Anne Spier was in charge of the Three Musketeers. Mary Anne is Kristy's best friend. I like her a lot. (But not as much as I like Kristy.)

"What do you guys want to do today?" she asked Hannie and Nancy and me.

"Can we go out in a boat?" asked Hannie.

"Can we go swimming?" asked Nancy.

53

"Can we explore?" I asked. "Please, please, purr-etty please?"

"Yes," Mary Anne answered. "But I can't do all three things at once. Nancy, why don't you go with Kristy? Hannie, why don't you go — "

"No!" I shrieked. "The Three Musketeers do everything together. We cannot split up. Then we would not be three. We have to stay in a bunch."

"We-ell," said Mary Anne.

"I know!" I cried. "This morning we will explore. This afternoon we will go swimming, and maybe ride in a boat. Okay?"

"Okay," said Hannie and Nancy and even Mary Anne.

We left the cabin. We walked around the porch until we were facing the woods. Then we ran into the backyard. We stopped and listened. It was very quiet. I could hear water lapping and birds chirping, but those were quieter noises than Stoneybrook noises. No cars or horns or garbage trucks.

"Let's take a walk in the woods," I said to Nancy and Hannie.

I guess my friends and I were moving faster than Mary Anne was. Because when we reached the woods, she was not with us. Oh, well. I could still see our cabin. We were not going to go very far. Mary Anne would catch up with us later.

You will never guess what we found in the woods. A secret house with a secret garden. Yup. That is true. We were just walking along when I saw some wood and stones. "Look over there!" I said.

"It's a house!" exclaimed Hannie.

"Is anyone home?" called Nancy.

No one answered her. We tiptoed closer to the little house. (It was more like a shed.) We peeped in a window. No one was home. The door was missing, so we crept inside. The little room was dark and damp.

"This could be our secret house," I whispered.

"We could fix it up," added Hannie. "For us and for the Doll Sisters."

"Hey, come here!" shouted Nancy. She was outside the house. "I found an old garden. Come look at it! It is extra-beautiful."

The garden *was* extra-beautiful. A lot of weeds were growing in it, but so were some other plants. Purple and yellow flowers were in bloom.

"We can fix up the garden, too," I said.

So we set to work. We worked until we heard Mary Anne calling us. Then it was time to leave the woods and our secret place.

12

Nancy

The Rainy Day

I felt *very* homesick at Shadow Lake. Not the whole time, just the first few days. I decided not to tell Karen and Hannie, though. I am not sure why. I know they are my friends, and friends share secrets. I guess I did not want them to think I was a baby. Anyway, the homesick feeling went away slowly. Maybe because I called Mommy and Daddy two times.

During the first week at the lake, the Three Musketeers did lots of things. We played outdoors every day. We fixed up a secret house and secret garden. We swam in the lake. We walked to a little store and bought penny candy.

One day after we had been at the cabin for a week, it began to rain. Karen and Hannie and I could not play outdoors. We had to stay inside with everyone else. The twenty of us sat around in the living room. Of course, the Three Musketeers sat together. We sat in a row on the floor. The Doll Sisters sat next to us.

Here is the funny thing, though. My friends and I were sitting together, but we were not playing together. We were not even talking. Karen was helping Andrew read some words in *Hop on Pop*. Hannie was making little people out of clothespins. And I was reading.

At least, I had been. Now I was just gazing around the room. I could not concentrate on my book. Sam and Charlie were playing chess. They were having a loud argument. Hannie was snapping her clothespins open and shut. Emily Michelle was playing with a talking doll, David Michael was playing with a paddle and ball, and Linny was making a set of clicker-clackers go clicketing away. Even the grown-ups were not quiet. They were rattling the newspapers they were reading.

I began to think of my house back in Stoneybrook, my quiet house, the one that three quiet people live in. In my house, I can always find peace. And I can always be alone, if I want.

I was a little teensy bit tired of living with so many people. I decided I was glad I was an only child. When I returned home, I could have my privacy back. I would not have to stand in line to go into the bathroom. I would not have to listen to chess arguments about pawns. I could read a book without hearing *Hop on Pop* in the background.

Why, I wondered, had I ever wanted a baby brother or sister?

I sighed. I stretched.

"You are taking too long with your

move!" Sam said to Charlie.

"Very good, Andrew!" exclaimed Karen.

Snap, snap, snap went Hannie's clothes-pins.

Rustle, rustle, rustle went the newspapers.

"My name is Cindy!" squealed Emily's doll.

I sighed again. I tried to read some more. After a long time, I heard Karen cry, "Hey, everybody! Look outside! The rain has stopped."

Everyone looked. The rain *had* stopped. The sun was even trying to shine. It made the drops of water on the leaves sparkle.

"Okay, Musketeers. Let's go outside," said Karen. "Bring the Doll Sisters. First we will go to our secret house. Then we will take a swim. Then . . ."

Hannie

The Big Dance

My Sari vacation went by too fast. In no time at all we were packing up to leave Shadow Lake. We were going back to Stoneybrook the next day. But before we left, one more fun thing would happen. We were going to a big dance at a lodge. Everybody had been invited — grown-ups, kids, anyone at Shadow Lake. (Well, not pets. Boo-Boo and Shannon were not invited, but I did not think they would mind.)

I was excited. Going to a dance meant getting dressed up.

"Look, Kristy," I said to Karen's big sister. Everyone was getting ready for the dance. I had just put on my special blue dress.

"That is lovely, Hannie," said Kristy, "but my mom said the dance is casual."

"Huh?"

"It is not a fancy dance. You do not need to dress up. People will be wearing blue jeans and shorts and stuff."

"Oh." I looked at Nancy and Karen.

"Bummer," said Nancy.

"Bullfrogs," said Karen.

They had wanted to get dressed up, too. But when we left for the dance with Karen's family and their friends, I was wearing my Minnie Mouse shorts and shirt, Karen was wearing leggings and a T-shirt, and Nancy was wearing jeans and a T-shirt.

We walked to the lodge. The lodge was a big building where people could meet. We had eaten at the restaurant there lots of times. Now we went into the big dance room. It was decorated with balloons. Along the walls were tables of food. A band was playing. A woman was singing.

I grinned at Nancy and Karen. "Awesome!" I exclaimed. Then I added, "I think this is a very grown-up dance. It is a good thing we went to dancing school, Karen. We will have to remember how to curtsy and use our manners, and especially how to waltz and do the foxtrot."

Guess what. One kind of dancing we did not learn at school was square dancing. At the lodge that night, everyone went do-si-do and swung their partners and did something that sounded like "almond right" and "almond left." I had lots of fun even though I did not know what I was doing.

Every now and then my friends and I got tired of dancing. Then we would take a break. And eat. On the tables were pies and cakes and cookies and fruit and punch and sodas. I ate a little bit more than I meant to.

I got a tummy ache. (A small one.)

So I sat down for awhile. I watched my friends.

"May I have this dance?" Karen asked Nancy. They waltzed around the room, even though no one else was waltzing.

For some reason, I thought about Sari then. Maybe because the last time I had a tummy ache, Sari came into my room. She sat with me on my bed. She patted my hand and sang, "She'll Be Comin' Round the Mountain." Except that Sari always sings, "We'll be bumpin' round a mountain when we come."

I watched Nancy and Karen dance. I watched Emily and Sam dance. Sam held Emily in his arms and whirled her around. Sari likes Linny and me to dance with her that way. She throws her arms out and laughs.

Soon the dance at the lodge was over. We walked home. I decided I would not *really* mind going home the next day.

KAREN

Carnival Time

Our trip to Shadow Lake went by in a big whoosh. It was over much too soon. Before we knew it, Andrew and I were back at the little house. That was on Saturday.

On Sunday, Hannie and Nancy and I played with the Doll Sisters. Then we rode our bikes around. Then we went to the playground.

On Monday, I telephoned Nancy early in the morning. "Come over and bring Merry," I told her. "We will make doll clothes."

"Okay," said Nancy.

Then I telephoned Hannie. "Come over and bring Kerry. We will make doll clothes," I said.

"I can't," answered Hannie.

"You can't bring your doll?"

"No. I cannot come over. Not today. I am going shopping with Mommy and Linny and Sari. Then we are going to a movie."

Well, for heaven's sake. I could not believe my ears.

"What about the Three Musketeers?" I said.

"What about them?"

"We are supposed to be together."

"We were together yesterday," said Hannie. "And for two weeks at the lake. And even before that. Even in school."

"We are supposed to be together *all the time*."

"We will be together tomorrow. Today I am going shopping."

"Okay, 'bye." I hung up the phone.

When Nancy came over with Merry, I said, "Hannie is going shopping today. With her mother and Linny and Sari."

"Not with us?" asked Nancy.

"No," I said. I made a Very Cross Face.

Nancy and I played all day. We made beautiful outfits for Merry and Terry. But Hannie was not with us, so we were not the Three Musketeers.

Guess what. At dinner, Seth said, "The carnival is in town. Who wants to go? We can go tonight."

"I do!" shrieked Andrew and I.

So Seth took us to the carnival. We brought Nancy along. We rode on the Ferris wheel. We walked through a spook house. (Andrew cried.) We looked at ourselves in wobbly mirrors. We ate cotton candy. We played games. (Andrew won a stuffed cow.) We had a gigundoly fun time.

But I was still cross with Hannie.

Nancy
Dapper Dan's

*R*ing, ring.

"I'll get it!" I called. "I'll get it, Mommy!" I had just finished my breakfast. I had eaten alone because Daddy had already gone to work, and Mommy was busy in the laundry room. I reached for the phone. I was pretty sure Karen was calling with her plans for our day.

"Hello?" I said.

"Hello . . . is this Nancy?" someone asked.

Mommy and Daddy say never to answer

yes or no to that question, especially if you are at home alone. Just say, "Who is calling, please?"

"Who is calling, please?" I said.

"It's Carly. Nancy?"

"Carly!" I cried. Carly is a friend I met in Hebrew school. I had not seen her since summer vacation began.

"Hi, Nancy! Guess what. My big sister is taking me out to lunch today." (Carly's big sister is in college or something.) "She said I could invite a friend. We are going to eat at Dapper Dan's. Do you want to come with us? We will have a really fun time."

I wanted to go to Dapper Dan's very badly. I wanted to see Carly. I wanted to meet her big sister. I was pleased that Carly had called. But do you know what I said to Carly? I said, "Oh, *thank* you! I want to go but I cannot. I have other plans."

I knew Karen would call soon. She would have plans for the Three Musketeers. I remembered when Hannie had gone shopping with her family. Karen had been *so*

71

angry. She had talked about that for days.
I mean, she had talked about it with everyone except Hannie. For a long time, Karen
would not speak to Hannie.

"Okay," said Carly. She sounded sad.

"Maybe I can go another time," I suggested.

"Maybe. But my sister does not take me
out to lunch very often."

"Oh."

When Carly and I finished talking, I hung
up the phone. It rang again right away. I
picked it up and said, "Hi, Karen."

"How did you know it was me?" she
asked.

"Just lucky."

"Well, guess what the Three Musketeers
are going to do today. We are going swimming. Melody Korman invited us over."
(Melody lives across the street from Karen's
big house.)

"Okay," I said.

"You do not sound very excited."

That was because I wasn't. "Sorry," I said.

"Well, put on your suit. Mommy will drive us to Melody's."

Hannie and Karen and I spent most of the day at Melody's house. My friends played Marco Polo. I sat at the edge of the pool. I thought about Carly.

My friends practiced diving. I floated on a raft. I remembered the chocolate milkshakes you can order at Dapper Dan's.

My friends took turns doing cannonballs. I lay on a towel by the pool. I wondered if Carly had invited another girl to lunch.

I felt cross all day.

"Hey, Nancy!" called Karen. "Don't you want to play? What's the matter?"

"NOTHING!" I shouted.

73

Hannie

The Three Enemies

*S*nap, *crackle, pop*. Linny and Sari and I were eating Rice Krispies for breakfast.

"I wonder why the cereal people spell so many words wrong," said Linny. He was reading the Rice Krispies box.

"What do you mean?" I asked.

"Well, like this. You don't spell 'crispy' with a K. You spell it with a C. And Corn Chex should be Corn C-H-E-C-K-S, I think. And — "

The phone rang.

"Oh, no," I moaned.

"What's wrong?" asked Linny.

"I know who is calling," I replied. "Karen."

"So?"

"So I don't know," I said, even though I did know. Karen was calling with plans for the Three Musketeers. And guess what. I was sick and tired of Karen and Nancy. I had spent nearly every single day of the summer with them. I had barely seen my other friends. I had not had enough time to read my library books. I had even checked out *Sarah, Plain and Tall* two times, and still I had not finished it. Plus, Mommy and Daddy had bought an ice-cream maker and I had not been able to help make ice cream.

Linny answered the telephone. "For you, Hannie," he said. He was frowning.

I took the phone from him. "Hi, Karen."

"Hi! Today we are going to make lemonade," she said. "We can sell it."

I paused. I thought about running a lemonade stand. Then I thought about *Sarah,*

Plain and Tall and the ice-cream maker. "Sorry," I said to Karen. "I cannot play with you today."

"Again?" cried Karen.

"This is only the second time."

"So what?"

"I will tell you so what," I said. "I am tired of you, Karen. How is that? I am tired of Nancy, too. I do not want to be a Musketeer today. I want to read and make ice cream and — and play with someone else!"

"Fine," Karen shouted. "Then *you* call Nancy and tell her that yourself."

"All right, I will."

"Good."

"Good-bye!" I slammed down the phone. Then I picked it up and called Nancy.

"Hi, Karen," she said. She did not sound very happy.

"It is not Karen. It's me, Hannie," I told her. "And guess what. I do not want to play with you and Karen today."

"You do not have to be so mad," Nancy answered. "Anyway, I do not want to play with you and Karen today, either. I am going to call Karen and tell her that. So there."

"So there too!"

Nancy and I hung up on each other. I stalked out of the kitchen. I went to my room. I looked at *Sarah, Plain and Tall*. I picked it up. Then I put it down again. I did not want to read it when I was in a bad mood.

I lay on my bed for awhile. I stared out the window.

"Hannie?" called a small voice. I turned around. Sari was at my door. "Will you play with me?" she asked. She held out a bunch of old dolls.

"Sure," I said.

Sari dumped her dolls on my bed. We played with them all morning. In the afternoon we played tag and Candy Land with Linny. Then we read some stories together.

Sari was good company. She helped me forget that the Three Musketeers were the Three Enemies now.

KAREN

Good News

I do not like to be mad at my friends. I do not like my friends to be mad at me. I mean, I *really* do not like those things. Hannie and Nancy were not talking to me and I was not talking to them. We had not talked to each other for one whole week. Do you know how hard that is? I just love to talk. When I couldn't talk to Hannie and Nancy, then I had to talk to Andrew and Emily Michelle and Emily Junior and our other pets. Talking to them is okay, but not the same as talking to my friends. The pets cannot even answer me, for heaven's sake.

I really missed Hannie and Nancy. I wondered if they missed me, too.

One Saturday, Andrew and I were at the big house. I was feeling sad. I was mad at my friends. Plus, I had not broken my dressing record yet.

"You are moping around," Kristy said to me.

"I know." I was lying on the couch. I was not doing a thing.

"Are you still mad at Hannie and Nancy?"

"Yup."

"Why don't you go over to Melody's?"

I shook my head. I *wanted* to go to Melody's, but I was afraid Hannie might be over there. What would I do if I saw her?

"Can I play with you?" I asked Kristy.

"Well, I would *like* to play, Karen, but I cannot. I am going over to Mary Anne's house. We are — "

"Can I come with you?"

"We are going to the mall. We are going to buy new tapes."

"I want to come."

"Karen, you always get bored in The Music Corner. You hate that store. And we are not going anywhere else."

"Boo," I said. "Bullfrogs."

A little while later, Kristy left. I sat in the living room and stared out the window. Soon Andrew sat next to me. He was holding *Hop on Pop*. "Let's read, Karen," he said.

I sighed. "Okay. First I will quiz you." I took the book. I opened it to the middle. "What is this word?" I asked.

Andrew peered at the page. He said the word.

"Good!" I cried. "What is this word?" I turned the page.

Andrew said the next word right, too.

I turned to another page. Before I could say anything, Andrew read the first word. Then he read the one next to it, and the next and the next until he had finished the page.

"Andrew! Oh, my gosh!" I shrieked.

"What? What? Did I make a mistake?"

"No! Andrew, you are reading! You can read!"

"I can?"

"Yes! Let's start at the beginning of the book."

Andrew read *Hop on Pop* all by himself from the beginning to the end. When he finished, I hugged him. Then I ran yelling through the house. "Andrew can read! Andrew can read!"

Everybody was very proud of Andrew. And everybody gave him more hugs. "Wait until Kristy comes home, Andrew! She will be proud of you, too," I said.

I ran into the kitchen. I had to spread the news to my friends. I reached for the phone, and . . . uh-oh.

I could not call Nancy and Hannie. They were my enemies, not my friends. They would not care about good news.

Nancy

Big Sister

While Karen was moping around the big house, Hannie was moping around *her* house, and I was moping around *my* house.

What a dull, boring Saturday, I thought.

I was lying on the couch in the family room. My feet were bare. I was bouncing them off the back cushions. Bounce, bounce, bounce.

"Nancy?" said Mommy.

Quickly I put my feet down. Mommy sat on the end of the couch. Daddy came into the room. He sat on the other end of the couch.

"Sit up for a minute, sweetie," Mommy said. "Daddy and I want to talk to you. We have something to tell you."

I sat up. Probably they were going to tell me to put my shoes on and start acting like I was seven.

Mommy smiled at me. She put her arm around my shoulders. "I have good news," she said. "At least, I think you will like the news."

"Are we going to Disney World?" I asked. Maybe Mommy and Daddy were feeling sorry for me. Maybe they were going to surprise me with a vacation.

"No," answered Mommy. "You are going to be a big sister, Nancy. I am going to have a baby. I'm pregnant."

"A baby? You are? I'll be a sister? Oh, wow!" My thoughts and words were all mixed up. I could hardly believe my ears.

"We're glad you are happy," said Daddy. "We thought you might be."

"Oh, yes!" I had forgotten how I had felt

at Shadow Lake, when I just wanted peace and privacy. The last week had been *too* peaceful and *too* private. Without my friends it had been boring and lonely. But when I had a little sister or brother I would never be bored or lonely again.

"When will the baby be born?" I asked.

"Not for awhile," said Mommy. "Not for about five months."

"Five months! I can't wait five months!"

"Sorry," said Daddy. He smiled.

"Can I plan the baby's room?" I asked.

"You may help us. You may also name the baby. Of course, we will have to agree to the name."

My mouth dropped open. This was better than a trip to Disney World.

"Oh, thank you, thank you!" I cried. I hugged Mommy. I hugged Daddy.

And then I called Karen on the phone. It was the only thing to do.

"Karen!" I exclaimed. "It's me, Nancy. Please do not hang up. I am sorry about the fight. *Very* sorry. And I do not want to be mad anymore. Guess what. My mother is going to have a baby!"

Karen gasped. "Oh, my gosh. You are going to have a little brother or sister, just like you always wanted! Hey, Nancy. I have great news, too. Maybe you could come over. Do you think someone could drive you to the big house? I will call Hannie now. I will tell her I am sorry. Then she can come over, too."

Before I knew it, the Three Musketeers were at the big house. We were very happy to see each other. I told Hannie my news. Then we ran out to Karen's backyard. We sat in the grass by a flower garden.

"Together again," said Karen, looking at Hannie and me.

"Let's always be best friends," said Hannie.

"Yes," I agreed. "But let's say that we do not have to be together every single second. And we can have other friends. But *we* will be *best* friends. There will never be any other Three Musketeers."

86

"Deal," said Hannie and Karen.

"Hey, Karen, what is your great news?" I asked.

"Andrew learned how to read," she answered. "Today he read *Hop on Pop* all by himself. You want to hear him?"

Of course we did. So Andrew read to us. To the Three Musketeers who were together again.

Hannie

Matthew or Dana

Ding-dong! rang the doorbell.

"I get it!" called Sari. She ran down the hallway.

"No, Sari. You are too little," I said. I ran after her. Sari and I reached the door at the same time. Sari could not turn the knob. "Anyway, they are *my* friends. I should get to open the door," I said.

Sari pouted. "Meanie-Hannie."

"I don't care if you call me names. Names do not bother me. Go find Mommy. Maybe she will give you a cookie. And Sari, you can*not* come to my slumber party. It is only for big girls."

"Meanie-Hannie," said Sari again. She walked away.

I opened the door. Nancy and Karen were standing outside.

"Hi, Musketeers!" I said. "Come on in."

The Three Musketeers were going to have a sleepover at my house. Our fight was finished. We had been friends again for an entire week.

"Let's go to my room," I said. I helped Nancy and Karen lug their knapsacks and sleeping bags upstairs. They spread them on the floor. I put mine on the floor, too. I could have slept in my bed, of course. But a sleepover is more fun when everyone is crowded onto the floor.

I closed the door to my room. "Ah, privacy," I said.

My friends and I played and played. Nancy and Karen had brought Merry and Terry with them. We decided the Doll Sisters should put on a show, so we made them perform the story of "The Three Billy Goats Gruff."

When the play was over, Karen held up a piece of paper. She said, "Look what I found. I found it in a magazine. It is a friendship test. You answer these questions. Then you score yourself. The score tells you if you are good friends or great friends or not-so-good friends or maybe enemies."

"Cool!" I said. Karen and Nancy and I each took the test. Our scores were very high. They meant that we were "close, loyal friends for life." We were sure that was true, even though we had to make up about half the answers. For instance, we do not know a thing about cars, so we just had to guess at the answer to: *Your friend asks if she may borrow your car. You say yes. Later, she calls to say that the fan belt broke. What do you do?* We did not know what a fan belt was, or why anyone would wear one, or if the

car was supposed to wear it, or what. So we just said we would forgive and forget. That seemed friendly.

We had to stop playing for awhile at dinertime. Mommy and Daddy made us eat with the family. But afterward, we were allowed to take Popsicles back to my room.

While we slurped away, Karen said, "Nancy? Are you still thinking about what to name the new baby?"

Nancy nodded. "Yup. Matthew or Dana. Definitely Matthew or Dana."

I giggled. "What happened to Biff Bartholomew or April May?"

"That was last week. I keep changing my mind."

"You know what name I like?" said Karen. "Roxanne. Isn't that beautiful?"

"I like Jilly," I said. "Or Tom for a boy."

"Jilly," Nancy repeated. "Jilly Dawes. That is a very nice name. Okay. Matthew or Jilly. Definitely Matthew or Jilly."

The door to my room opened then. Sari

walked in. She had just barged in without even knocking. *"Sari!"* I yelled.

Sari smiled at me. She was wearing her nightgown. She was ready for bed. "Night-night, Hannie," she said. She blew me a kiss. Then she left.

I turned to Nancy. "I hope you get a sister just like Sari," I told her.

KAREN

Best Friends

I was watching Hannie's chest move up and down, up and down. She sleeps very heavily. Every now and then she would snore a little. Her snore sounded more like a snort, though.

I rolled over and looked at Nancy. I think maybe she was dreaming. Her hands and her mouth were moving just a little bit.

I coughed. I wanted my friends to wake up. The sun was shining. It was time to go outside and play. Also, I was hungry. I wanted breakfast.

Our slumber party was almost over. Soon Nancy and I would leave Hannie's house. But in three days we were going to have another sleepover. This one would be at the little house.

Snort! snorted Hannie. She woke herself up.

I giggled. "Hey, Hannie. You snore!" I whispered.

Hannie looked horrified. "I do not!"

"Do too," said Nancy. (Her eyes were not even open yet.) "Actually, you snort. Like this." Nancy opened her eyes. Then she began snorting. She did not stop until Hannie threw a pillow at her.

We were all laughing. "I am so glad we are friends again," I said.

"Me too," agreed Nancy and Hannie.

The Three Musketeers crawled out of the sleeping bags. We got dressed. We went downstairs to eat breakfast.

Sari was in her high chair. "She waited for you," Hannie's mother said to us. "She wants to eat with the big girls."

Hannie did not get mad. She just smiled.

We were finishing our breakfast when the phone rang.

"Hannie, it's for you!" called Linny. "It's a . . . boy!"

"Probably Timmy Hsu," she said.

She was right. Timmy is a very good friend of Hannie's. He lives down the street.

Hannie talked to Timmy for a few minutes. Then she said, "I will call you back, okay?" Hannie hung up the phone. She looked at Nancy and me. "Um, Timmy wants me to come over and play. What should I tell him? What are the Three Musketeers going to do today?"

Nancy's face reddened. She began to look uncomfortable. "I was going to go back to my house. And then I was going to eat lunch at Dapper Dan's. With Carly. She invited me again after all."

"Melody asked me to go swimming," I

admitted. "I thought it would be okay. I did not know we were going to spend today together, too."

"I guess we aren't!" said Nancy. "Hannie's going to Timmy's, you are going to Melody's, and I am going out to lunch with Carly."

"And that is okay, right?" asked Hannie.

"Fine with me," I said. "We are still best friends, still the Three Musketeers. And we are going to have another sleepover soon."

"Goody," said Hannie. She called Timmy back to tell him she could play.

Nancy said, "Lunch is going to be really fun. I did not tell Carly and her big sister about the baby yet. They will be so happy to hear about Bugsy or Sweetpea." Nancy folded her napkin carefully.

"Bugsy or Sweetpea?" I yelped.

Nancy grinned. "Just kidding. But I *have* changed the names again. I will call the baby either Amber or Brad."

"No. If you get a sister, name her Karen, after me!"

"I think the baby should have a name all her own. Or all his own," said Nancy.

"Well, you don't need to decide right away," I said. "Today we have too many other things to think about. Come on. Let's go."

The Three Musketeers got ready to spend the day with their other friends.

Activity Pages

Hooray! Summer is finally here. That means no school and no homework! But if you are left with nothing to do, never fear — the Three Musketeers are here. And they have plenty of games and projects for you to try. Turn to page 137 for answers to the puzzles if you get stuck.

Three Cheers for the Musketeers!

Summer has begun. And Karen, Hannie, and Nancy are going to spend their vacation together. After all, they *are* best friends. How many words can you make from the letters in the word FRIENDSHIP? To start you off, each of the Musketeers has made a word for you.

FRIENDSHIP
ride
rip
hen

Friendship Bracelets

The Three Musketeers wear friendship bracelets to show they are best friends. Here's how to make bracelets for you and your friends. Remember: these bracelets are tricky to make. You may not get it right the first time, but keep trying. Best friends are worth the effort! Follow the pictures. They will help you.

You will need:
4 pieces of brightly colored embroidery thread — 1 yard each

Here's what you do:
1. Tie the strings together in a knot about three inches from the top of the thread. This is the top of your bracelet.
2. Tape the top of the bracelet to a hard surface to make it easier to weave.

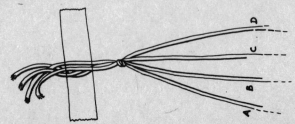

3. Pick up string A. Move it over and under string B and up through the loop you have created.
4. Tighten the knot by holding string B tight and pulling string A up.

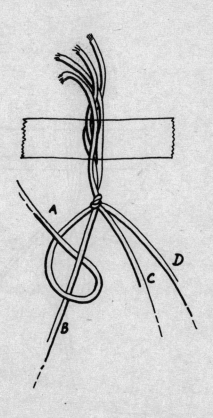

5. Drop string B. Pick up string C. Pull string A over and under string C, just as you did with string B, to make a knot.
6. Do the same thing using string A and string D. Now string A is on the right.

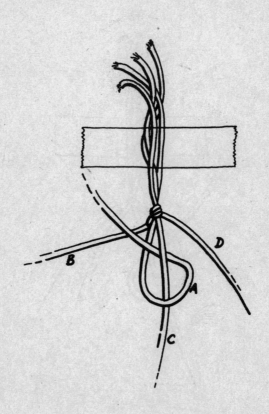

7. That is one row. Keep going, repeating steps 3 through 7, always starting with the string on the left.

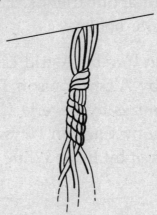

You can stop when the bracelet will fit over your friend's wrist with a little room to let it slip on and off. Don't forget to tie a knot at the end of the bracelet when you are finished!

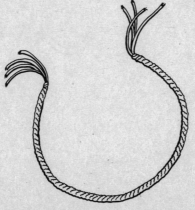

Books about Friendship

Karen *loves* to read. And she especially loves to read about friends. Here are some of her favorite books.

Pippi Longstocking by Astrid Lindgren
Lad, a Dog by Albert Payson Terhune
Henry and Beezus by Beverly Cleary
B is for Betsy by Carolyn Heywood
Charlotte's Web by E. B. White

Popsicle Stick Boxes

Need a place to store your secret stuff? Why not store it in your own Popsicle stick box? Here's how to make a box just like Karen, Hannie, and Nancy made.

You will need:
50 Popsicle sticks
white glue

Here's what you do:
1. Place two sticks a few inches apart as you see in the picture.

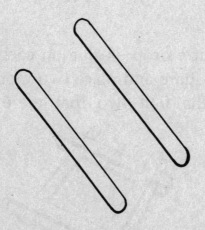

2. Put a drop of glue on the ends of each stick.
3. Place two more sticks on top of the two with the glue so that they form a square. Be sure to press the ends so the glue will stick.

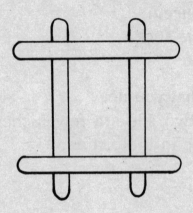

4. Now put a drop of glue on each corner of the square and place two more sticks above the first two that were placed down.

5. Repeat step 4, changing the direction of the sticks, and build up until the box is as high as you would like it to be.
6. To make a flat lid for your box, lay out a line of Popsicle sticks side by side on the table. Glue them together in a straight line as you see in the picture.
7. To make a handle for your lid, cut two Popsicle sticks in half. Glue the halves one on top of the other. Then glue the handle to the lid of your box. Voilà!

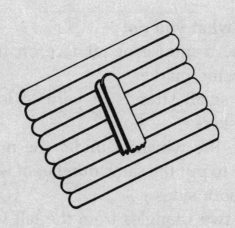

Pet Rocks!

Mom and Dad say you can't have a live pet? Well, how about a pet rock? Here's how to make one that looks like Karen's pet rat, Emily Junior!

You will need:
a gray rock
a permanent marker
pink felt
thin yarn
white glue
scissors

Here's what you do:
1. Draw a mouse or rat face on the rock with the marker.
2. Cut small strands of yarn to look like whiskers.
3. Glue the whiskers under the nose. (Be sure to put the same number of whiskers on both sides.)
4. Cut two triangles from the felt for ears.

5. Glue the ears on the rock.
6. Cut four small pink ovals for feet from the felt.
7. Glue the felt feet to the bottom of the rock.
8. Cut a long strand of yarn for the tail.
9. Glue the yarn to the back of your rock to make your pet complete. Don't forget to name your pet rock rat!

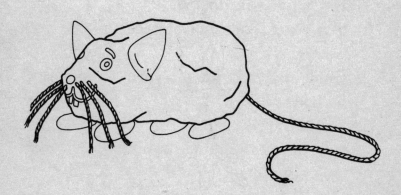

Hannie's Clothespin People

Hannie makes dolls out of clothespins and other things she finds around the house. You can make clothespin people, too. It's easy. All you need are some old fashioned wooden clothespins, glue, some pieces of material, some small household objects, and a lot of imagination. Before you know it, you'll have a whole town of clothespin people.

Use a permanent marker to draw a face on your clothespin. Now dress her up! Cut material and wrap it around for a dress. A button makes a smashing hat! Scraps of lace make wonderful scarves. Beads and string can make beautiful necklaces. For a more adventurous clothespin person, use aluminum foil to make a super space age astronaut's space suit. Aluminum foil can also be rolled up to make antennae for alien clothespin people. Just paint your clothespin green and glue on the antennae. Be creative. There are millions of people to make from clothespins.

Papier-Mâché Balloon Heads

If two heads are better than one, why not make a spare? (Remember: making papier-mâché can be messy, so do this outside.)

You will need:
a round balloon
a safety pin
newspaper
a bowl
2 cups of water
1 cup of flour
tempera paints
paint brushes

Here's what you do:
1. Tear the newspaper into strips.
2. Blow up the balloon.
3. Mix the flour and water together in the bowl. Stir until smooth.
4. Take a strip of paper, drag it through the flour mixture until soaked, and wrap the strip around the balloon.

5. Continue to wet and wrap strips until the balloon is completely covered, except for the knot, with a few layers of paper.
6. Set aside to dry. This may take a while!
7. When the papier-mâché is dry, use the safety pin to pop the balloon. Pull the balloon out of its shell. You will be left with a hard head.
8. Use the paint and brushes to paint a face on your head. You can even glue yarn on the head for hair. Be creative!

Summer Fun Wordsearch!

When Karen's around, summer days are packed with summer fun. Can you find words that stand for summer fun in this puzzle? They go up, down, sideways, diagonally, and backwards. Look for: COOKOUT, FAIR, CANOE, BIKE, HIKE, FISH, TENNIS, ROW, CLIMB, PLAYGROUND, SKATE, CAMP, READ, SWIM, DIVE, BASEBALL.

```
C F G S T R U P M N
O A R L B B E L C D
O I N S I M N A X R
K R N O K D M Y D A
O L T F E P G G S L
U Z E K I H B R K E
T E N N I S S O A V
L S R O W J H U T I
F I A I C H P N E D
B B M I L C T D C S
B A S E B A L L S Z
```

Let's Go to the Playground Maze!

There are always lots of gigundoly exciting things going on at the playground! Karen can't wait to get there. Hop on your bike and follow her through the maze.

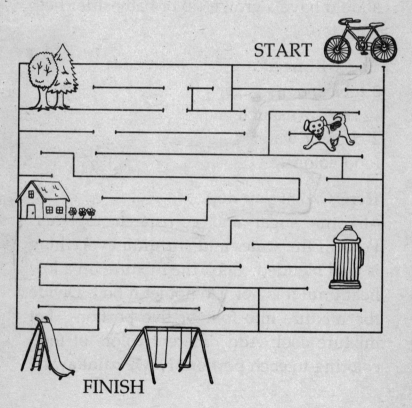

START

FINISH

Finger Fun!

Karen and Andrew love to spend their time making messy finger paintings. Here's an easy recipe for your own finger paints! Kristy helps Karen make the paints. You should have a grown-up or baby-sitter help you, too.

You will need:
3 tablespoons sugar
½ cup cornstarch
2 cups of water
food coloring

Here's what you do:
Mix the sugar and cornstarch together. Pour in the water and stir until everything is well blended. Cook the mixture on a low heat until it is hot. Do not let it boil. Divide the mixture into four or five portions. Let mixture cool. Add different colors of food coloring to each portion. Now, paint away!

All that Glitters Glitter Paintings

These paintings really shine!
To make glitter paintings, use your regular tempera paint to paint a picture. Before the paint dries, sprinkle glitter wherever you'd like. The paint will glue the glitter to the paper when it dries.

Terrific Travel Games

Unfortunately, sometimes summer vacation can mean spending a lot of time in the car. Here are two games that will help pass the time as the miles fly by.

The Pass Along Story

Find a piece of paper and a pencil. Write down the first two or three lines of a story. Then fold down the paper and pass it to the next person. No fair peeking! Let everyone in the car play (except the driver, of course). If you want the story longer, keep passing the paper. Now read the story out loud. You're sure to laugh it up!

Dots

To play this paper and pencil game, start by drawing rows of dots like you see in the picture.

Now the fun begins. The first player draws a line anywhere — either up, down, or sideways, from one dot to the one next to it. The next player does the same thing. The object of the game is to draw a line that will complete a box. If you draw the last line on any box, the box is yours. Put your initial inside it. When all the boxes have been completed, the game is over, and the person with the most boxes is the winner.

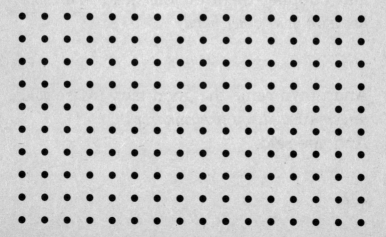

Silly Songs!

The Three Musketeers never tire of singing silly songs. These two are gigundoly silly — and guaranteed to make you giggle all through any car trip!

Little Rabbit Foo Foo

This song has silly hand motions, too. Follow the directions on this page.

(Sing)

Little Rabbit Foo Foo *(Make rabbit fingers)*
Hopping through the forest,
Scooping up the field mice *(Use your hand as a scooper)*
and bopping them on the head! *(Hit your fist with your other hand)*

(say)

And down came the good fairy *(Make your fingers come down like raindrops)*
And she said,

Little Rabbit Foo Foo, *(Make rabbit fingers)*
I don't want to see you *(Make your finger move in a no-no movement)*,
Scooping up the field mice
and bopping them on the head. *(Same as before)*

(say)

I'll give you three more chances and then I'll turn you into a goon! *(Make your scariest face!)*

(Repeat the song three times. Then add:)

(sing)

Little Rabbit Foo Foo,
I didn't want to see you
Scooping up the field mice
and bopping them on the head.

(say)

I gave you three chances
and now I'm turning you into a goon!

And the moral of the story is:
Hare today: goon tomorrow!

John Jacob Jingleheimer Schmidt

As you and your best pals sing this silly song, make your voices get quieter and quieter each time around. Then after you have sung at a teeny tiny whisper, shout the verse one last time at the top of your lungs!

John Jacob Jingleheimer Schmidt,
His name is my name, too!
And whenever we go out
The people always shout
There goes John Jacob Jingleheimer Schmidt
La la la la la la la!

Rainy Days

When it rains, the Three Musketeers never get bored. They're full of rainy day ideas!

Rainy Day Recipes

When the rain comes, Karen loves to make these simple treats, just for Andrew. (Of course she eats a little bit, too!)

Cream Cheese Carrots

You will need:
3 ounces cream cheese
2 shredded carrots
1 cup shredded cheddar cheese
2 teaspoons honey
8 sprigs of parsley
waxed paper

Here's what you do:
Allow the cream cheese to soften in a mixing bowl. Stir in the honey and cheddar cheese with the cream cheese. Add one shredded carrot. Chill the mix for 45 minutes.
Roll the chilled mix into carrot-shaped sticks. Spread the leftover carrot shreds onto waxed paper. Roll the sticks in the shreds. Lay the carrot-covered sticks out on

waxed paper. Add a parsley sprig to the wide end of each carrot. These treats are beautiful, healthy, *and* delicious.

Super-Duper Ice-Cream Soup!

Here's a sweet soup that's easy to make and delicious to slurp!

You will need:
your favorite ice cream
chocolate chips (or any candy or cookie that you love!)
banana slices
whipped cream
hot fudge
bowl
wooden spoon

Here's what you do:
Spoon a couple of scoops of your favorite ice cream into the bowl. Add the chocolate chips, banana slices, hot fudge, and whipped cream. Now use the spoon to stir the ice cream and toppings. When they are

all mixed together, and the ice cream has softened into a soupy mess, drink up. It tastes soup-er!

Carnival Candy Apples

A candy apple a day keeps the frowns away. (But be sure to make these sweet treats with the help of an adult.)

You will need:
1¼ cups sugar
1 cup light corn syrup
6 hard apples
6 ice-cream sticks
red food coloring
measuring cup
wooden mixing spoon
waxed paper
medium sized cooking pot
candy thermometer (You *must* have one of these.)

What you do:
1. Mix the sugar with the corn syrup.
2. Cook the mixture over a low flame. Stir until the mixture starts to boil.
3. Let the mixture heat until the thermometer says 300° F.

4. While the mixture is cooking, stick an ice cream stick into each apple.
5. Spread waxed paper on the counter.
6. When the mixture is ready, turn off the heat and stir in a few drops of red food coloring.
7. Hold each apple by the stick and dip it into the mixture. When the apple is covered with candy, place it stick up on the wax paper.
8. When the candy apples cool, take a bite!

YUMMM!

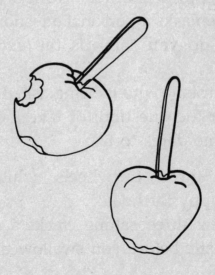

Super Sleepover Ideas!

Everyone knows nobody sleeps at a sleepover! So here's some stuff you can do while you're staying awake!

Truth or Dare!

Nancy, Karen, and Hannie love this game. Do you dare to try it with your friends?

Here's how to play:

You and your friends sit in a circle. One friend says to another "Truth or Dare . . ." and then asks a personal question, such as, "Who do you think is the cutest kid in class?"

The friend who is being asked can either answer the question, or take a dare. Here are some dares to try:

1. Do three cartwheels while singing "Happy Birthday."
2. Chew three saltine crackers and try to whistle before you swallow them.

3. Hop on one foot and sing "Take Me Out to the Ball Game."
4. Skip backward around the room while saying your name — backward.

Memories!

Karen will never forget the sleepover she had with all of the girls in her class. How good is your memory? Here's a game you and your friends can play to test your memory power.

Spread a collection of objects on a tray. You can include things such as hairbrushes, pencils, stuffed animals, magazines, or any funny things you can find.

Try and put at least 15 objects on the tray. Let everyone in the room stare at the tray for several minutes. Then take the tray out of the room.

Now give everyone a piece of paper and a pencil. Put on your thinking caps and write down everything you remember seeing on the tray. The person who writes down the most correct things, wins!

Friends Forever! *Charmane*

How well do you know your best friends?
Take this simple quiz and find out.

1. What color are your best friend's eyes? *Brown*
2. What is your best friend's favorite TV show? *full house*
3. Who is your best friend's favorite teacher? *farlan*
4. What is your best friend's favorite book? *The roky montin*
5. Which of the Three Musketeers is your best friend's favorite? *Henny*
6. On a rainy day, what does your best friend do for fun? *rains*
7. On a sunny day, what does your best friend do for fun? *out side*
8. What is your best friend's most prized possession? *()*
9. When is your best friend's birthday? *octh*
10. If your best friend could meet anyone in the world, who would it be? *DJ*

Now you can check your answers with your friend.

133

- If you got eight or more answers correct, you are such a good friend that Karen has made you an honorary member of the Three Musketeers.
- If you got six or seven answers correct, you are a terrific listener who tries to learn all she can about her pals.
- If you got three, four, or five answers correct, you are the type of person who loves to be around a lot of friends all at once. But that makes it hard to keep all of your best friend's likes and dislikes fresh in your mind.
- If you got less than three answers correct, ask your mom if your best friend can sleep over tonight — you guys have some catching up to do!

Old Time Silent Movies!

Hooray for Hollywood! You and your sleep-over friends can pretend to make old-time silent movies at home. All you need are a few flashlights.

One of you gets to be the movie star. The others get to work the lights. While the star moves around (without talking, this is a silent movie, don't forget!) the rest of you follow her around with the flashlights. Blinking the flashlights on and off really fast makes the "star" look as if she is in an old-time silent movie! Take turns being the star — after all, anyone who likes Karen is a star in her book!

Make Your Own Nonsense Stories

Karen hopped happily around the blue sidewalk and Hannie did handstands on her vanilla bicycle.

If that sentence doesn't make sense to you, then you've never made up Nonsense Stories! Nonsense Stories use silly sentences. Here's how to make up your own.

Prepare your stories before your sleepover starts. First, make up a short story. Now erase one or two words in each sentence. In the place of the missing word, write down what kind of word it is. Here's an example. "Karen walked the frisky puppy down the road," becomes "(Name) walked the (description) puppy down the (object)."

Before reading any of your story, ask your friends to give you the missing words. For example, "Give me a name, a description, and an object." When the words are all filled in, read the story out loud to everyone. What a laugh!

Puzzle Answers

Three Cheers for the Musketeers!

hip	shed
ship	send
pen	friend
den	rind
red	nip

What other words did you find?

Summer Fun Wordsearch!

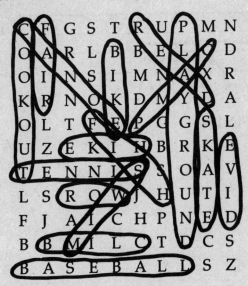

Let's Go to the Playground Maze!

START

FINISH

Enter the BABY·SITTERS Little Sister™

Perfect Day Giveaway!

Karen, Hannie, and Nancy are the Three Musketeers. They spent their perfect day together at Shadow Lake. Now you and your two best friends can win your own version of a "Perfect Day" (valued up to $250) as the Three Musketeers. Just fill in the coupon below and return it by November 30, 1992.

4 Grand Prize Winners!

Each grand prize winner receives $250 PLUS **3 personalized "Three Musketeers" t-shirts** — one for you and one for each of your two friends. The t-shirts will have your name and your two friends' names on them so everyone will know that you're the best of friends!

20 Second Prize Winners receive 3 personalized "Three Musketeers" t-shirts!

Rules: Entries must be postmarked by November 30, 1992. Winners will be picked at random and notified by mail. No purchase necessary. Valid only in the U.S. Void where prohibited. Taxes on prizes are the responsibility of the winners and their immediate families. Employees of Scholastic Inc.; its agencies, affiliates, subsidiaries; and their immediate families are not eligible. For a complete list of winners, send a self-addressed stamped envelope to Baby-sitters Little Sister Perfect Day Giveaway, Giveaway Winners List, at the address provided below.

Fill in the coupon below or write the information on a 3" x 5" piece of paper and mail to:
BABY-SITTERS LITTLE SISTER PERFECT DAY GIVEAWAY,
Scholastic Inc., P.O. Box 7500, Jefferson City, MO, 65102.

- -

Baby-sitters Little Sister Perfect Day Giveaway

I would spend my Perfect Day with (first name)_____
and (first name) _____.

We would spend the day: (check one)
- ❏ At the amusement park
- ❏ Shopping at the Mall
- ❏ Roller blading / roller skating
- ❏ Other_____
_____

Name_____ Age_____

Street_____

City_____ State_____ Zip_____

Where did you buy this *Baby-sitters Little Sister*™ book?
- ❏ Bookstore
- ❏ Book Club
- ❏ Drugstore
- ❏ Book Fair
- ❏ Supermarket
- ❏ Other_____(specify)
- ❏ Library

BLS192

Kristy is Karen's older stepsister, and she and her friends are...

by Ann M. Martin, author of *Baby-sitters Little Sister* ™